Are there real dragons?

Contents

Written by Sally Morgan
Illustrated by Laszlo Veres

Collins

What's in this book?

Listen and say 1

lizard
tongue
claws

Lily and Mum are watching the celebration. There's a big dragon. People are dancing. The dragon is moving up and down.

Dragon dance

Lily can see people. This dragon is not real.
"Are there real dragons?" asked Lily.

Dragons in China

People love dragons. There are many stories about dragons in China. People think dragons are good.

These dragons are like snakes with feet and big heads. They have long bodies.

Dragon boats

These are dragon boats. Can you see the dragon's head?

Dragon boats move fast in the water. But these dragons are not real.

Dragons in stories

There are lots of dragons in story books.

This dragon looks different from the dragons in China. It has a bigger body. It has big wings and it can fly. It has fire coming from its mouth!

Often these dragons are not nice! But they aren't real dragons!

But there are animal dragons in some places.

Komodo dragons

The Komodo dragon is very big! It is the biggest lizard in the world. It grows to three metres long.

Komodo dragons have a big head, four legs, a big body and a strong tail. They have strong claws, too. They haven't got wings so they can't fly.

Can you see its long tongue?

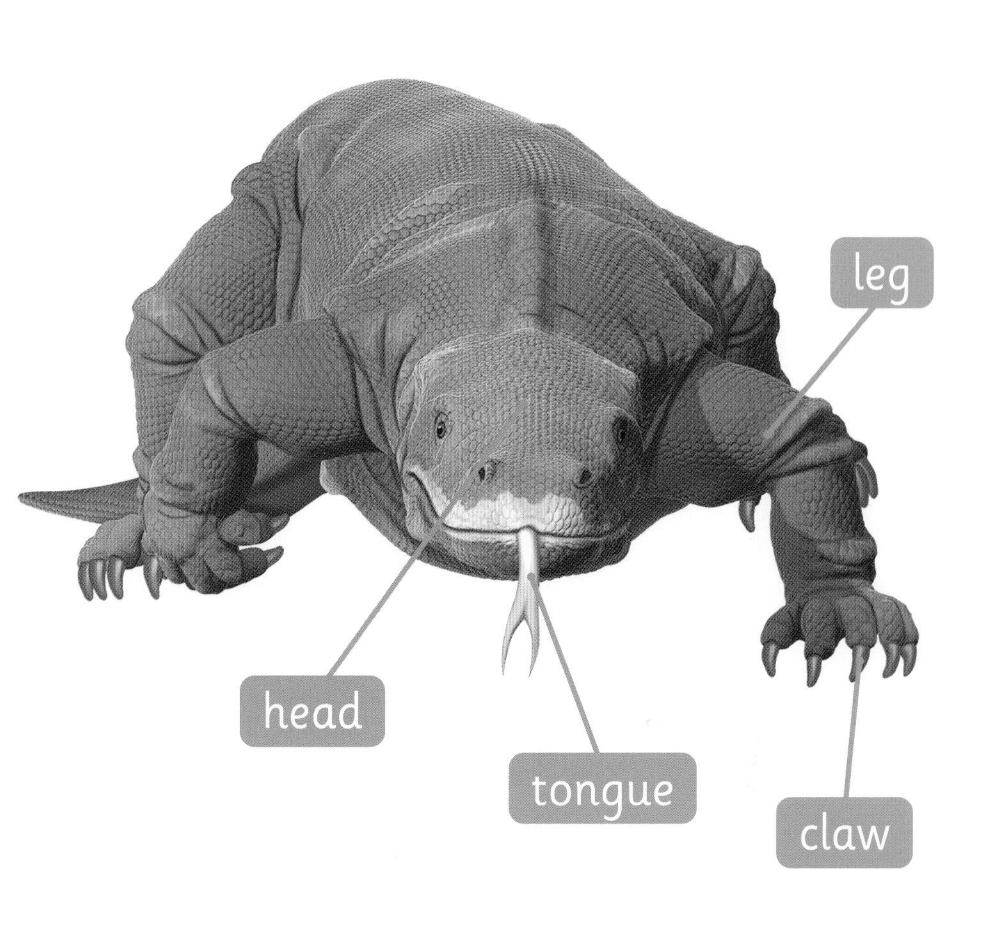

These dragons eat other animals.

Sea dragons

The leafy sea dragon is a fish. It lives in the sea. Do you think it looks like a fish or a dragon?

Seaweed is a plant. The sea dragon is hiding in the seaweed.

The dragonfish lives at the bottom of the sea. It is cold and dark there. It has a big head and long teeth. It eats small fish.

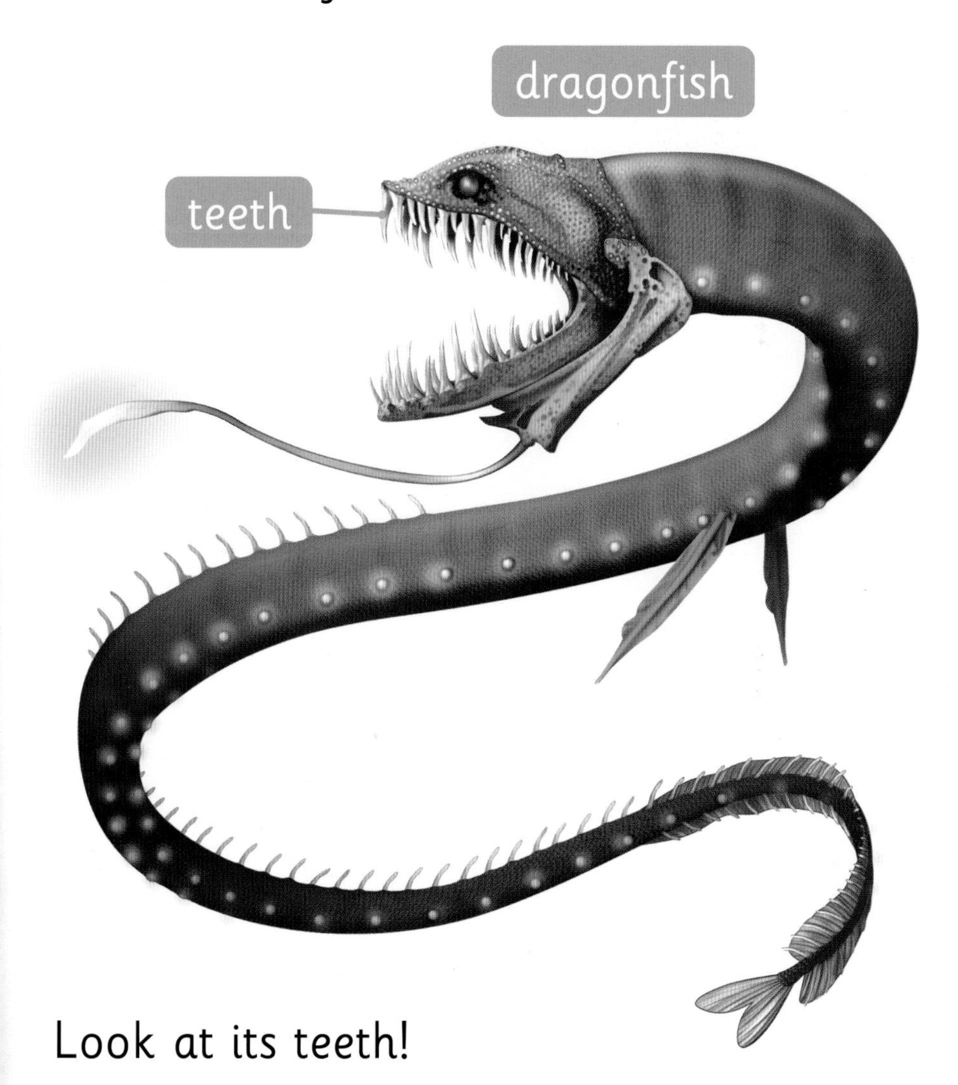

Look at its teeth!

Tree dragons

The flying dragon is a lizard. It lives on trees in hot, wet forests. It climbs up and down the trees very fast. It eats small animals like flies and spiders.

Sometimes, flying dragons jump off trees. They put their legs out and fly to the next tree.

Can you see its wings?

Flying dragons

Dragonflies live near water. They have four wings and they can fly.

Dragonflies catch and eat small flies.

Can you count its legs? How many legs has it got?

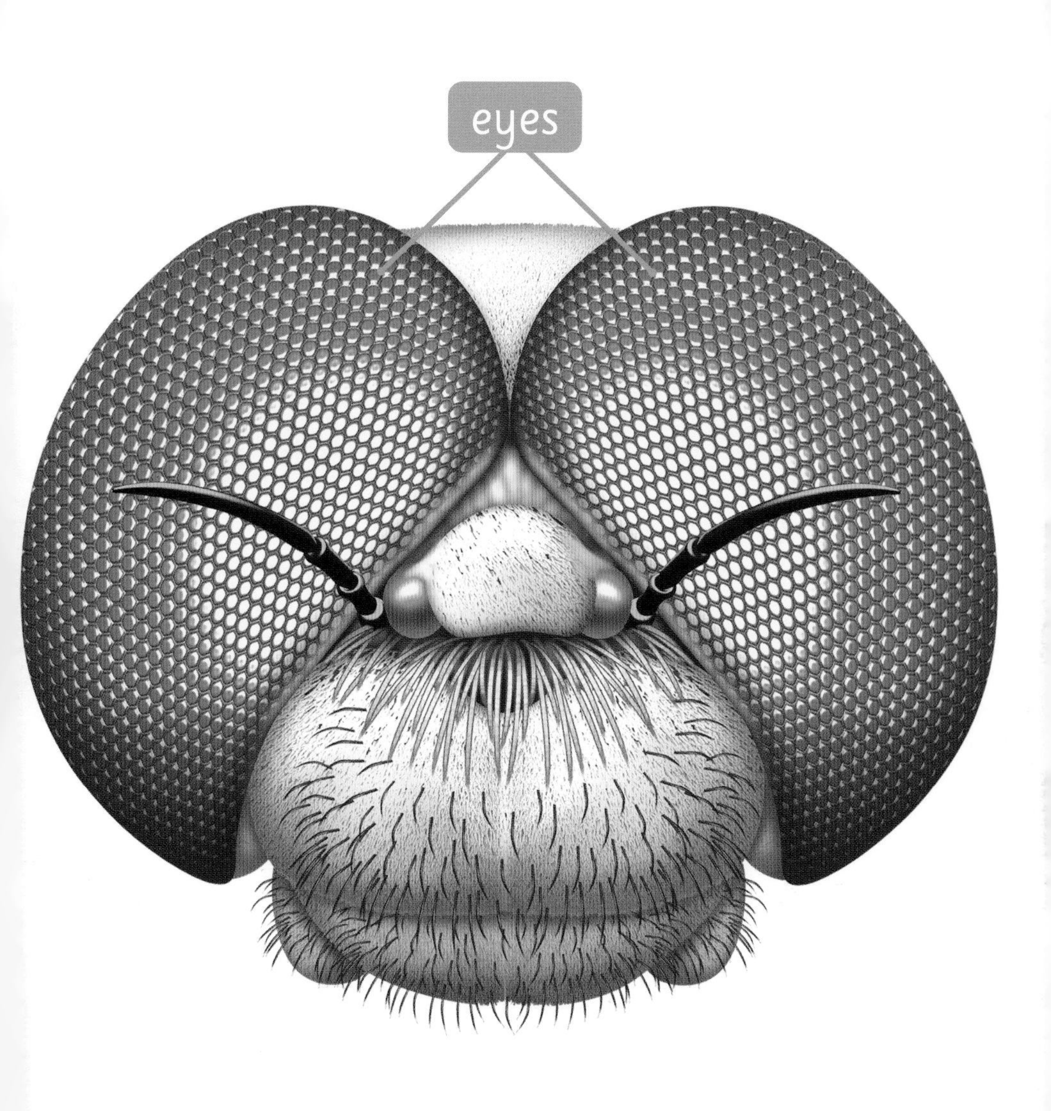

Dragonflies can see very well. They have two big eyes.

Water dragons

Water dragons have a long, green body and a tail. They are lizards. They climb trees and find food.

Water dragons like swimming.
Can you swim?

Paper dragons

You can make a paper dragon.
They're easy to make.

This is what you need.

This is how you make it.

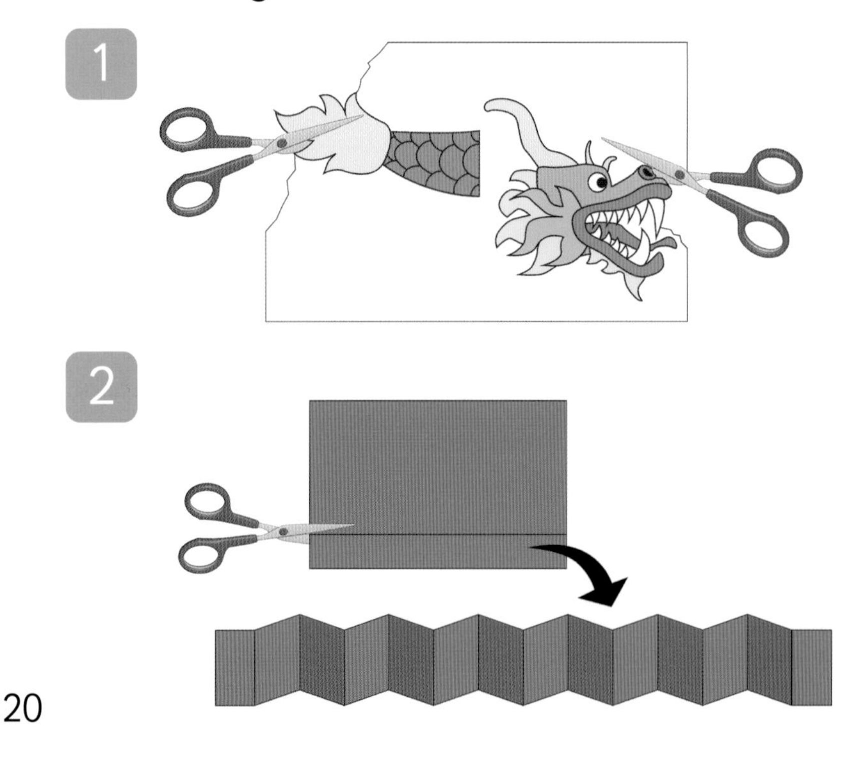

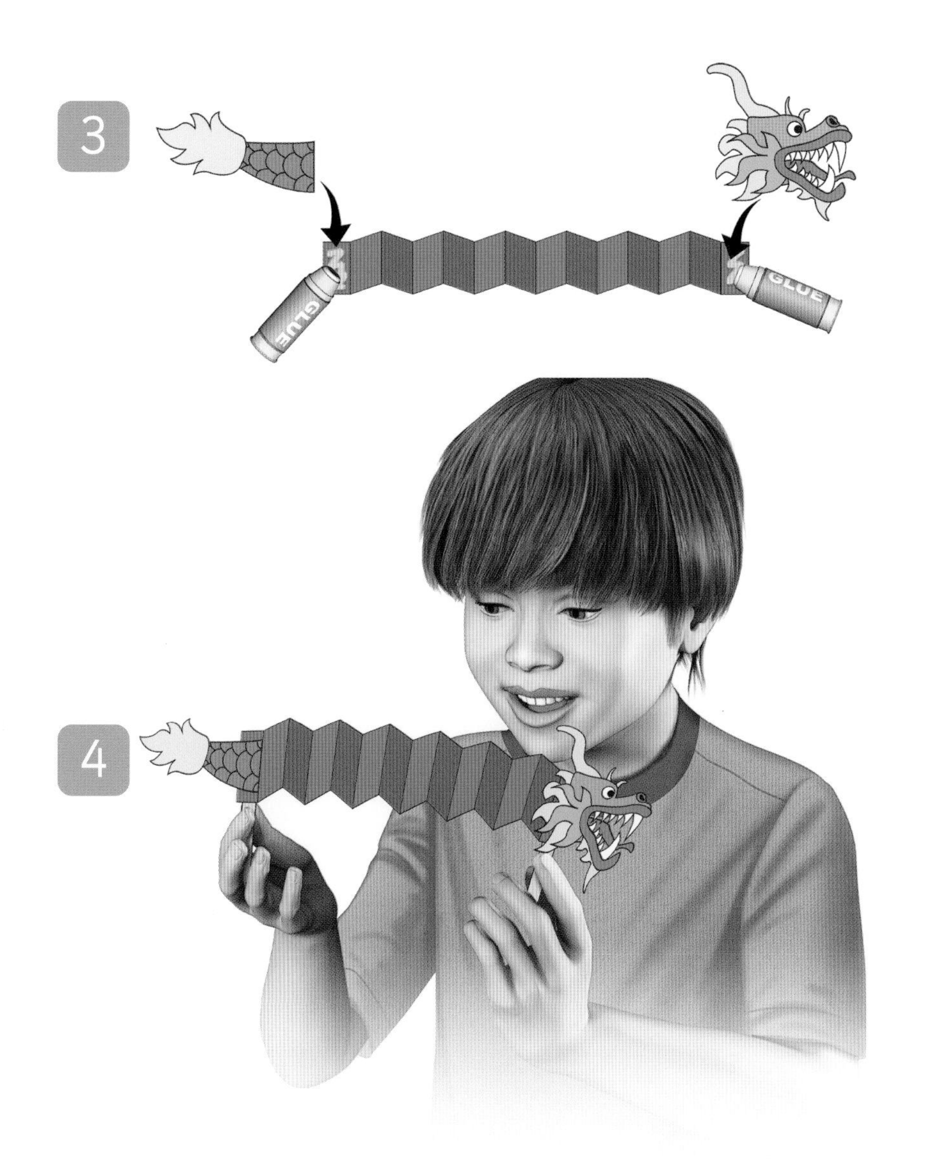

Now you know there are lots of different dragons. Some dragons are animals, some are in story books and some are paper.

Picture dictionary

Listen and repeat 3

1 Look and match

dragonfly

komodo dragon

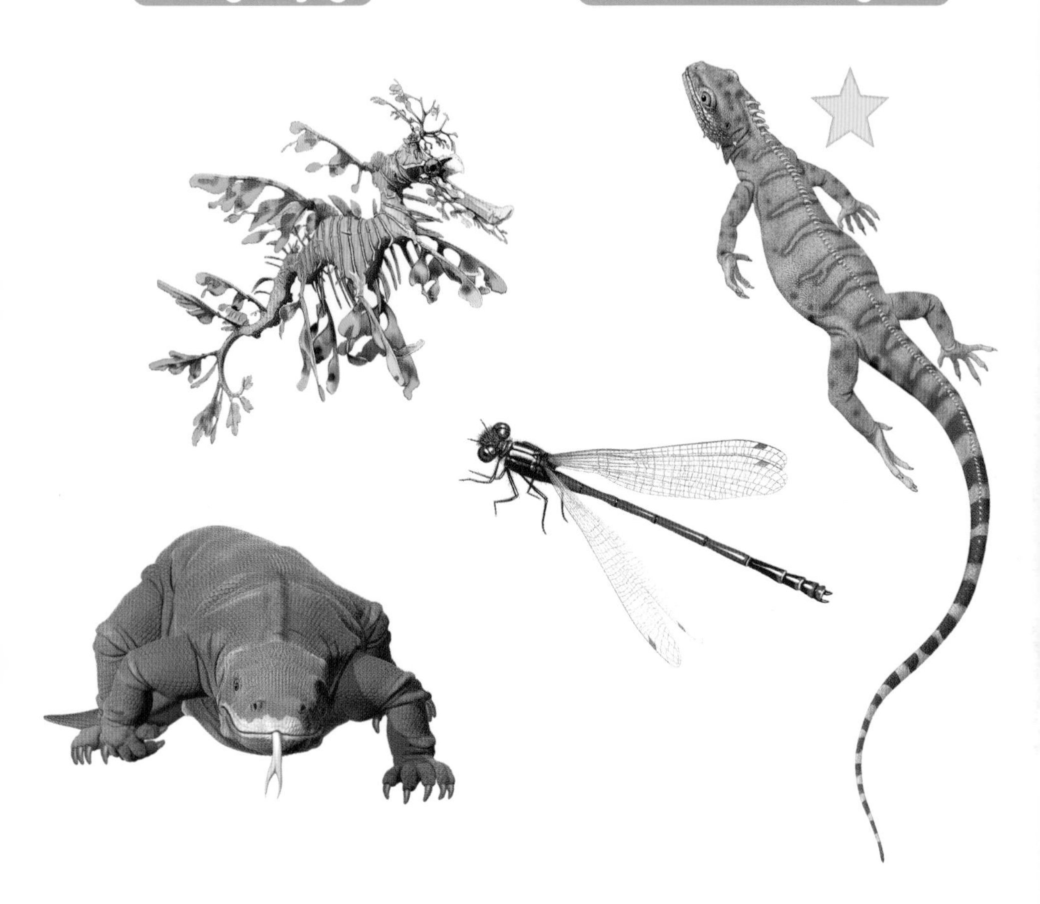

water dragon

leafy sea dragon

2 Listen and say  

Collins

Published by Collins
An imprint of HarperCollins*Publishers*
Westerhill Road
Bishopbriggs
Glasgow
G64 2QT

HarperCollins*Publishers*
1st Floor, Watermarque Building
Ringsend Road
Dublin 4
Ireland

William Collins' dream of knowledge for all began with the publication of his first book in 1819.

A self-educated mill worker, he not only enriched millions of lives, but also founded a flourishing publishing house. Today, staying true to this spirit, Collins books are packed with inspiration, innovation and practical expertise. They place you at the centre of a world of possibility and give you exactly what you need to explore it.

10 9 8 7 6 5 4 3 2

ISBN 978-0-00-839660-2

www.collins.co.uk/elt

British Library Cataloguing in Publication Data

A catalogue record for this publication is available from the British Library.

Author: Sally Morgan
Illustrator: Laszlo Veres (Beehive)
Series editor: Rebecca Adlard
Commissioning editor: Zoë Clarke
Publishing manager: Lisa Todd
Product managers: Jennifer Hall and Caroline Green
In-house editor: Alma Puts Keren
Project manager: Emily Hooton
Editor: Barbara MacKay
Proofreaders: Natalie Murray and Michael Lamb
Cover designer: Kevin Robbins
Typesetter: 2Hoots Publishing Services Ltd
Audio produced by id audio, London
Reading guide author: Emma Wilkinson
Production controller: Rachel Weaver
Printed and bound by: GPS Group, Slovenia

MIX
Paper from responsible sources
FSC™ C007454

This book is produced from independently certified FSC™ paper to ensure responsible forest management.

For more information visit: **www.harpercollins.co.uk/green**

Download the audio for this book and a reading guide for parents and teachers at www.collins.co.uk/839660